Sherlock Hemlock and the Creatures from Outer Space

by Ray Sipherd

Illustrated by Sammis McLean

Featuring
Jim Henson's Sesame Street
Muppets

A SESAME STREET/GOLDEN PRESS BOOK
Published by Western Publishing Company, Inc. in
conjunction with Children's Television Workshop.

One day, Sherlock Hemlock, the world's greatest detective, was sitting in his easy chair reading a book about outer space.

"...and on the planet Snarf lived strange creatures with incredible powers," he read. "The creatures were preparing to visit other planets— including EARTH!..."

"I'm glad this is only a story," Sherlock Hemlock said to himself. "If I were not a brave detective I would be very scared."

Suddenly he heard people shouting and running outside.

Sherlock Hemlock looked out the window and saw everybody running down the street.

"It's coming!" shouted Bert, as he looked up at the sky. "Hurry! Get inside!"

"Egad!" Sherlock Hemlock cried as he watched the people hurrying indoors. "Something strange is coming. Everybody is afraid and running away! What could it be?

"I have it! The creatures from SNARF are coming! Well, I, Sherlock Hemlock, will go out and find the creatures and scare them away!"

When Sherlock Hemlock went outside, Sesame
Street was empty. He didn't notice the black storm
clouds in the sky or the leaves shivering on the
trees or the branches waving in the wind.

He was too busy looking for the creatures from
outer space.

Then he heard a rumbling in the distance.

He hurried up to the roof of 123 Sesame Street and looked in all directions. The rumbling seemed to be coming closer. "Zounds!" cried Sherlock. "That noise must be the approaching spaceships!"

As he hurried back downstairs, the wind
began to WHOOSH down Sesame Street. Sherlock
Hemlock stopped and listened.
"Aha! That loud roar must be rocket engines.
The creatures from Snarf are landing in their
spaceship right here on Sesame Street!"

BAM! The door in the fence by Big Bird's nest
slammed shut. "That's where the creatures are
hiding!" Sherlock Hemlock said to himself.

But when he opened the door and
looked in the nest, nobody was there.

All at once flashes of lightning streaked across the sky and thunder boomed.

"Now the creatures are signalling to each other with their lights!" cried Sherlock Hemlock. "They are beating on their drums to scare me! But am I afraid?" he asked himself. "N-n-no!" he answered. "N-not fearless Sherlock Hemlock!"

The wind blew harder and harder. Empty cans rolled along the street, and leaves and papers flew past Sherlock Hemlock.

"Aha!" he shouted above the sound of the wind. "Now the creatures from Snarf are throwing things. They must be very angry! But I, Sherlock Hemlock, the world's greatest detective, will not run away!"

WHAM! Something round and hard and metal hit the great detective, knocking him flat.

"Just as I thought," said Sherlock, as he lay on the sidewalk. "I have been hit by a small flying saucer!"

"I will hide under this," said Sherlock, holding the saucer-shaped object over his head.

Just then hundreds of icy, round hailstones began falling from the sky.

"Gadzooks!" cried Sherlock Hemlock. "Now the creatures are throwing stones at me!"

Then it started to rain. But Sherlock Hemlock was
listening to something else now.

"Footsteps! I hear the creatures' footsteps coming
down the street. And they're coming toward *me* —
and getting closer . . . and CLOSER . . . and *CLOSER!*"

Suddenly he saw . . .

...two small children.

Their hair was windblown and their clothes were wet from the rain. They crowded under the lid with Sherlock. "May we get under here with you?" they asked.

"Egad!" cried Sherlock Hemlock as he looked at them. "Your hair is wild and both of you are dripping wet! *You* must be the creatures from Snarf!"

"We're not creatures from anywhere," the children told him. "We're Polly and Ned from down the street. The wind blew us, and the lightning and thunder scared us. The hailstones fell on us, and the rain got us all wet!"

"What's that?" asked Sherlock Hemlock. "You say there was wind? And lightning? And thunder? And hailstones? And rain?"

"Yes," said Polly. "We were caught in the big storm."

"*Wait!*" cried Sherlock. "I have the answer!"

"Listen everyone!" Sherlock Hemlock called. "Come out! There's nothing to be afraid of. There are no creatures from Snarf. There are just these two small children ... who were caught in a *BIG STORM!*"

So as the dark clouds passed and the sun shone again, Sherlock Hemlock, the world's greatest detective, went on his way, looking for another mystery to solve.